Dear Parent:

Congratulations! Your child is taking the first steps on an exciting journey. The destination? Independent reading!

STEP INTO READING® will help your child get there. The program offers books at five levels that accompany children from their first attempts at reading to reading success. Each step includes fun stories, fiction and nonfiction, and colorful art. There are also Step into Reading Sticker Books, Step into Reading Math Readers, and Step into Reading Phonics Readers— a complete literacy program with something to interest every child.

Learning to Read, Step by Step!

Ready to Read   Preschool–Kindergarten
• big type and easy words • rhyme and rhythm • picture clues
For children who know the alphabet and are eager to begin reading.

Reading with Help   Preschool–Grade 1
• basic vocabulary • short sentences • simple stories
For children who recognize familiar words and sound out new words with help.

Reading on Your Own   Grades 1–3
• engaging characters • easy-to-follow plots • popular topics
For children who are ready to read on their own.

Reading Paragraphs   Grades 2–3
• challenging vocabulary • short paragraphs • exciting stories
For newly independent readers who read simple sentences with confidence.

Ready for Chapters   Grades 2–4
• chapters • longer paragraphs • full-color art
For children who want to take the plunge into chapter books but still like colorful pictures.

STEP INTO READING® is designed to give every child a successful reading experience. The grade levels are only guides. Children can progress through the steps at their own speed, developing confidence in their reading, no matter what their grade.

Remember, a lifetime love of reading starts with a single step!

For Sue, Heather, and Drew.
And for Edy, who gave me the confidence
when I didn't know "Beans"!

www.stepintoreading.com

Educators and librarians, for a variety of teaching tools, visit us at
www.randomhouse.com/teachers

Library of Congress Cataloging-in-Publication Data
Torrey, Rich.
Beans Baker, number five / by Richard Torrey. p. cm. — (Step into reading. A step 3 book.)
SUMMARY: When he is given an unlucky uniform number, Beans Baker considers giving up baseball rather than face kidding from the other players.
ISBN 0-307-26335-5 (trade) — ISBN 0-307-46335-4 (lib. bdg.)
[1. Baseball—Fiction. 2. Self-confidence—Fiction.] I. Title. II. Step into Reading. Step 3 book.
PZ7.T64573 Be 2003 [E]—dc21 2002012954

Printed in the United States of America 13 12 11 10 9 8 7 6 5 4
First Random House Edition

STEP INTO READING, RANDOM HOUSE, and the Random House colophon are registered trademarks of Random House, Inc.

STEP INTO READING®

STEP 3

Beans Baker, Number Five

by Richard Torrey

Random House 🏠 New York

The first game of the season
was only three days away.
Coach Munhall was
handing out uniforms.

Beans could hardly wait.
All spring he had dreamed
of wearing number 21.
Just like his hero—
The Great Roberto.

Coach Munhall held up
the number 21 jersey.
"Here I am!" shouted Beans.
But Coach Munhall handed
it to Sheldon.
"There must be a mistake,"
Beans said.
"That's *my* number!"

"No," said Coach Munhall.

"Here's your uniform."

Beans looked at his jersey.

"Number five? IT CAN'T BE!"

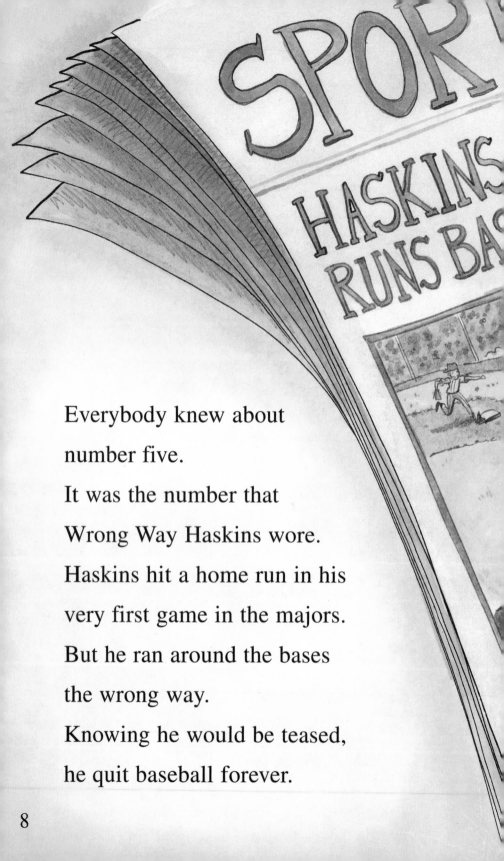

Everybody knew about
number five.
It was the number that
Wrong Way Haskins wore.
Haskins hit a home run in his
very first game in the majors.
But he ran around the bases
the wrong way.
Knowing he would be teased,
he quit baseball forever.

"Hey, Beans.
Make sure you don't put
that jersey on the *wrong way!*
Get it?"
Sheldon snickered.

"This is terrible,"
groaned Beans.
"I'm going to be laughed
out of town."
"It's just a number,"
said Coach Munhall.

11

At practice the next day,

Beans tried to hide his number

by wearing his jacket.

But it kept getting in the way.

It was his worst practice ever.

"Hey, Wrong Way.

Let me show you the *right* way!"

said Sheldon.

He hit a pitch out of the park.

"Reminds you of The Great Roberto,

doesn't it?"

Beans told his friends he was
thinking about quitting the team.
"But you love baseball," said Lindsay.
"Almost as much as me!"
Beans shook his head.
"I can't play wearing number five."

14

"It's just a number,"

Chester reminded him.

"It's Wrong Way's number!"

said Beans.

"I might as well be wearing number 13!"

"Hey, that's *my* number!" said Chester.

"Sorry," said Beans.

Beans didn't go to the next practice.

"I'm not feeling well,"

he told his mother.

He wasn't really sick.

But when he thought about

wearing number five,

he did feel a little queasy.

At practice, everyone wondered
where Beans was.
"We can't let him quit,"
Chester said to Lindsay.
"How can we stop him?"
"I have an idea," said Lindsay.
"Here's the plan...."

After practice, Chester and Lindsay

stopped at Beans' house.

"Guess what?" said Lindsay.

"We're quitting the team, too."

"*What?*" said Beans. "Why?"

"We don't want to get

teased," said Chester.

"With these glasses, who knows

what other teams might call me?

Four eyes. Goggle head..."

"Goggle head?" said Beans.

"There's no telling what kind of teasing a girl catcher might get," said Lindsay.
"Better safe than sorry. Right, Beans?"

"WRONG!" shouted Beans.
"Who cares what other teams say?
Chester, your glasses
help you see the ball better.
Lindsay, you're the best
catcher in the league!
And you *love* baseball—
almost as much as me!
You guys can't quit just because
people might laugh at you.
You're making a huge mistake!"

"I think you just talked us
      out of quitting," said Lindsay.

"I think I just talked *myself*
      out of quitting," said Beans.

"It worked!" shouted Chester.

"I mean—see you at
      the game, Beans!"

The next morning,
Beans and his family arrived
at the field just as the game
was about to start.
"You're late," shouted Sheldon.
"Did your dad go the *wrong way?*"

Coach Munhall made Beans
sit on the bench
because he had missed practice.
But he told him to stay ready.
Beans watched as the other team
went ahead, two to nothing.

Then, in the bottom
of the ninth,

Chester and Lindsay
both got hits.

With two outs, everyone
was counting on Sheldon
to hit a home run and
win the game.

"Come on, Sheldon!"

Chester yelled from second base.

"Just like in practice!"

"Only this time, it's for real!"

added Lindsay.

Sheldon's knees started to knock.

Even from the bench,

Beans could see his face turning white.

All of a sudden, Sheldon fainted!
He fell on top of the catcher.
R-R-R-RIP! went Sheldon's pants.
"Beans, you'll have to bat!"
yelled Coach Munhall.

29

"NOW BATTING—
BEANS BAKER, NUMBER FIVE!"
said the announcer.
Beans' family cheered.

The other team laughed.

"Number five? It's Wrong Way!"

they shouted.

Beans stepped up to the plate.

"Hey, Wrong Way.

Want a map?" the catcher said.

Beans swung at the first pitch.
He missed, and his
helmet spun around.

"Strike one!" shouted the umpire.

The other team laughed even harder.

"Look!" yelled the pitcher.

"He's wearing his helmet

the *wrong way!*"

Beans swung at the second pitch.

He missed again.

"Strike two!" shouted the umpire.

"Maybe he's holding the bat

the *wrong way!*"

the shortstop hollered.

Beans took a deep breath
and waited for the third pitch.

KLIP!

Beans hit a ground ball.

It skipped toward the first baseman.

"*I'm out*," thought Beans.

But the ball hit

the first baseman's knee

and bounced high in the air.

"Run!" shouted Coach Munhall.

Beans was already running,

rounding first base.

As the ball came down,
it hit the pitcher on the head
and bounced toward the outfield.
"Keep going!" shouted Coach Munhall,
waving his arm like a windmill.

Beans stepped on second base

and kept running.

The center fielder kept running, too—

right into the left fielder!

CRASH!

Chester scored!

Lindsay scored!

Beans tagged third base

and headed for home!

The left fielder picked up the ball
and threw it with all his might.
"SLIDE, BEANS, SLIDE!"
yelled Coach Munhall.

43

Beans, the catcher, and the ball
all arrived at the same time.
When the cloud of dust settled,
the umpire yelled, "SAFE!"

There was no more laughing.
There were no more
jokes about "Wrong Way."
Beans Baker, number five,
had won the game!
"Ice cream for everyone!"
shouted Coach Munhall.

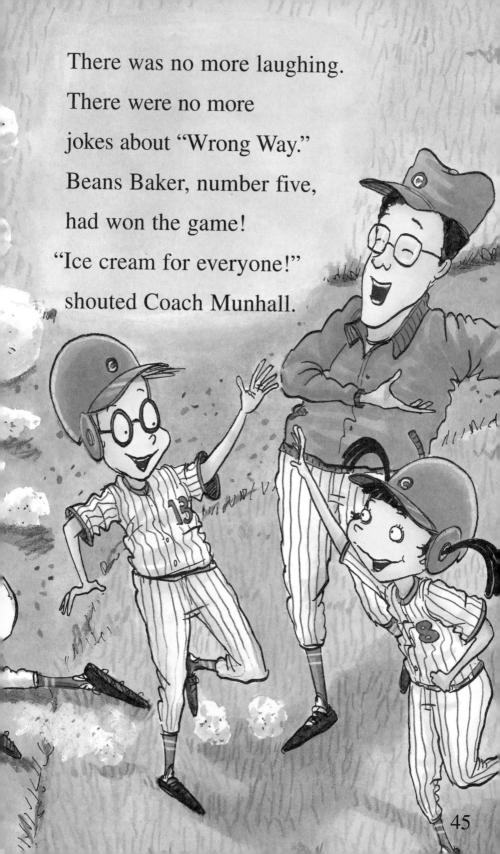

"Hey, Beans," said Lindsay.
"Sheldon said he doesn't want
The Great Roberto's
number anymore.
Everyone's calling him
The Great RIP-erto!"

"Now you can switch to number 21!" said Chester.

"No," said Beans.

"Five is fine with me. Besides—"